the **BAD GUYS**

EPISODE

13

CUT TO
THE CHASE

A SCHOLASTIC PRESS BOOK
FROM SCHOLASTIC AUSTRALIA

SCHOLASTIC PRESS
AN IMPRINT OF SCHOLASTIC AUSTRALIA PTY LIMITED
(ABN 11 000 614 577)
PO BOX 579 GOSFORD NSW 2250
WWW.SCHOLASTIC.COM.AU

PART OF THE SCHOLASTIC GROUP
SYDNEY • AUCKLAND • NEW YORK • TORONTO • LONDON • MEXICO CITY
• NEW DELHI • HONG KONG • BUENOS AIRES • PUERTO RICO

FIRST PUBLISHED BY SCHOLASTIC AUSTRALIA IN 2021.
TEXT AND ILLUSTRATIONS COPYRIGHT © AARON BLABEY, 2021.

NATIONAL
LIBRARY
OF AUSTRALIA

A CATALOGUE RECORD FOR THIS
BOOK IS AVAILABLE FROM THE
NATIONAL LIBRARY OF AUSTRALIA

ISBN: 978-1-76066-868-6 (PAPERBACK)

TYPESET IN JANSON, ELO, KERBEROS FANG AND BEHANCE.
DESIGN BY NICOLE STOFBERG.

PRINTED BY MCPHERSON'S PRINTING GROUP, MARYBOROUGH, VIC.
SCHOLASTIC AUSTRALIA'S POLICY, IN ASSOCIATION WITH MCPHERSON'S PRINTING GROUP,
IS TO USE PAPERS THAT ARE RENEWABLE AND MADE EFFICIENTLY WITH WOOD FROM
RESPONSIBLY MANAGED SOURCES, SO AS TO MINIMISE ITS ENVIRONMENTAL FOOTPRINT.

10 9 8 7 6 5 4 3 2 1   21 22 23 24 25 / 1

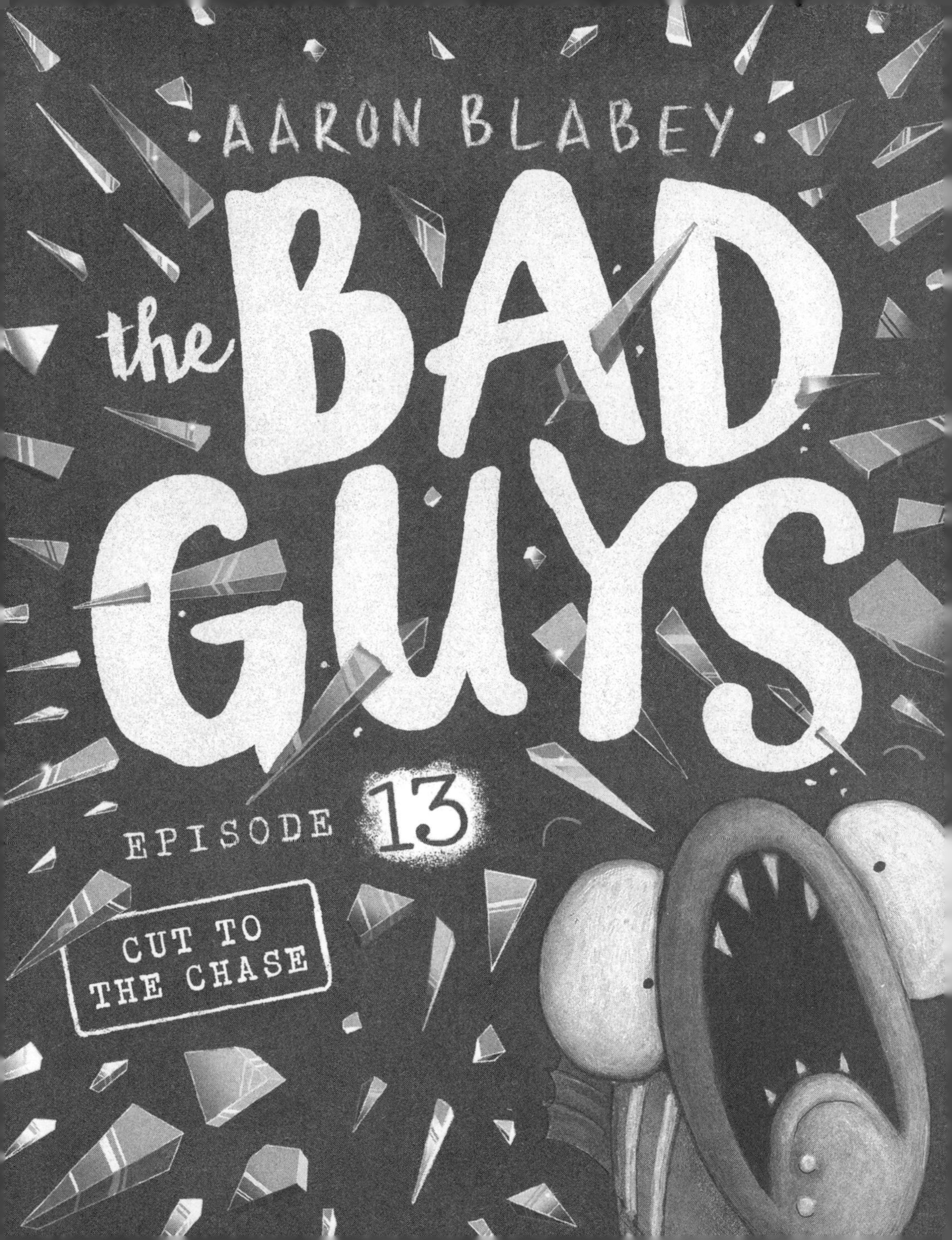
AARON BLABEY
the BAD GUYS
EPISODE 13
CUT TO THE CHASE

Ugly Snake!

Ugly Snake!

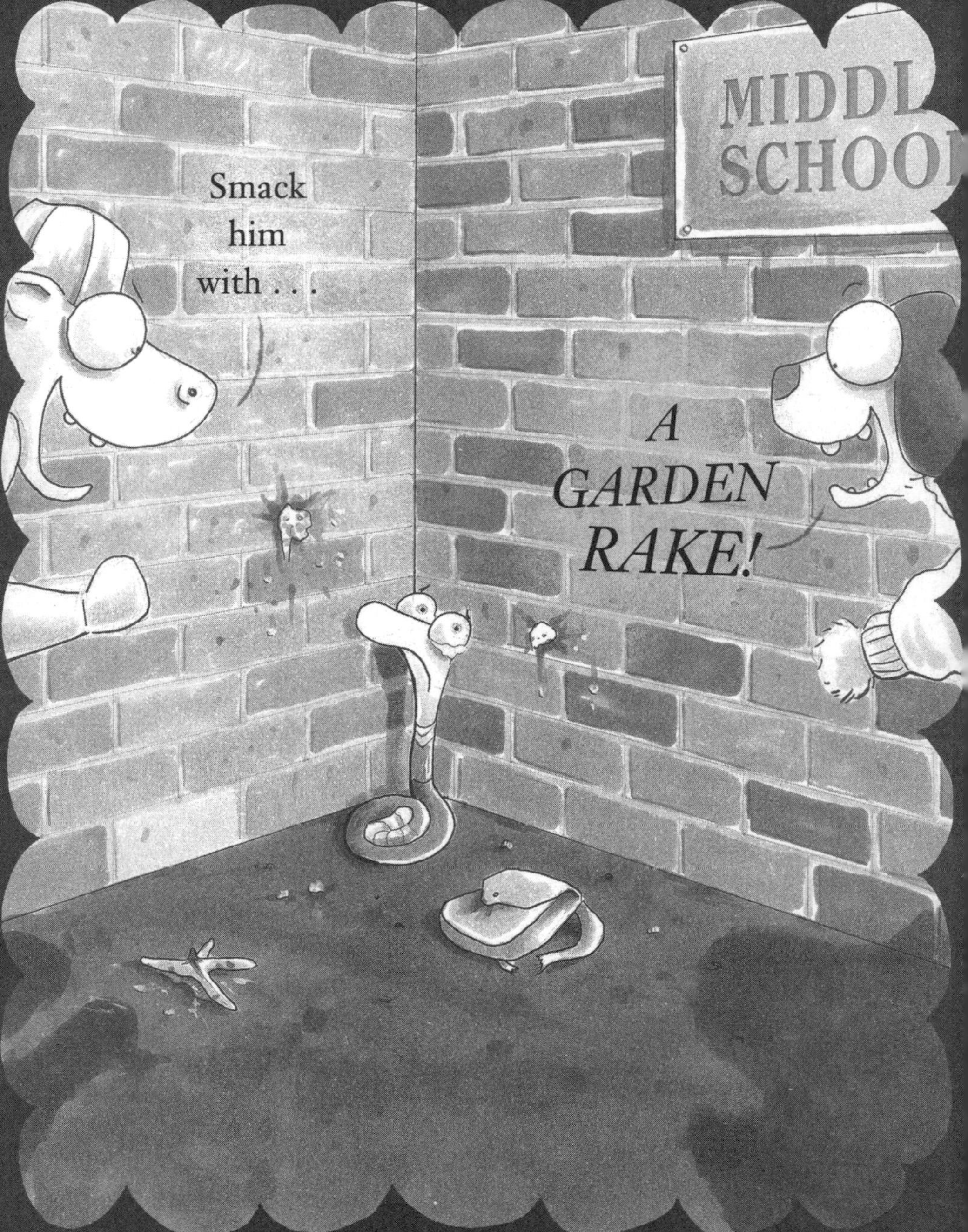
MIDDL
SCHOO
Smack him with . . .
A GARDEN RAKE!

· CHAPTER 1 ·
FORGET WHAT YOU KNOW

KITTY!

I can't

slow us

down!

This isn't HOT POOP STORAGE!

I WANT HOT POOP STORAGE!

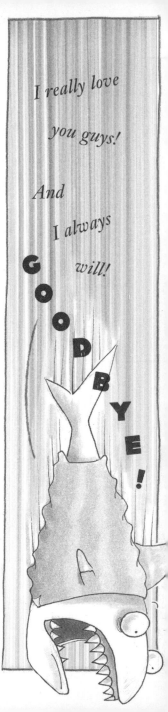

I really love you guys!

And I always will!

GOODBYE!

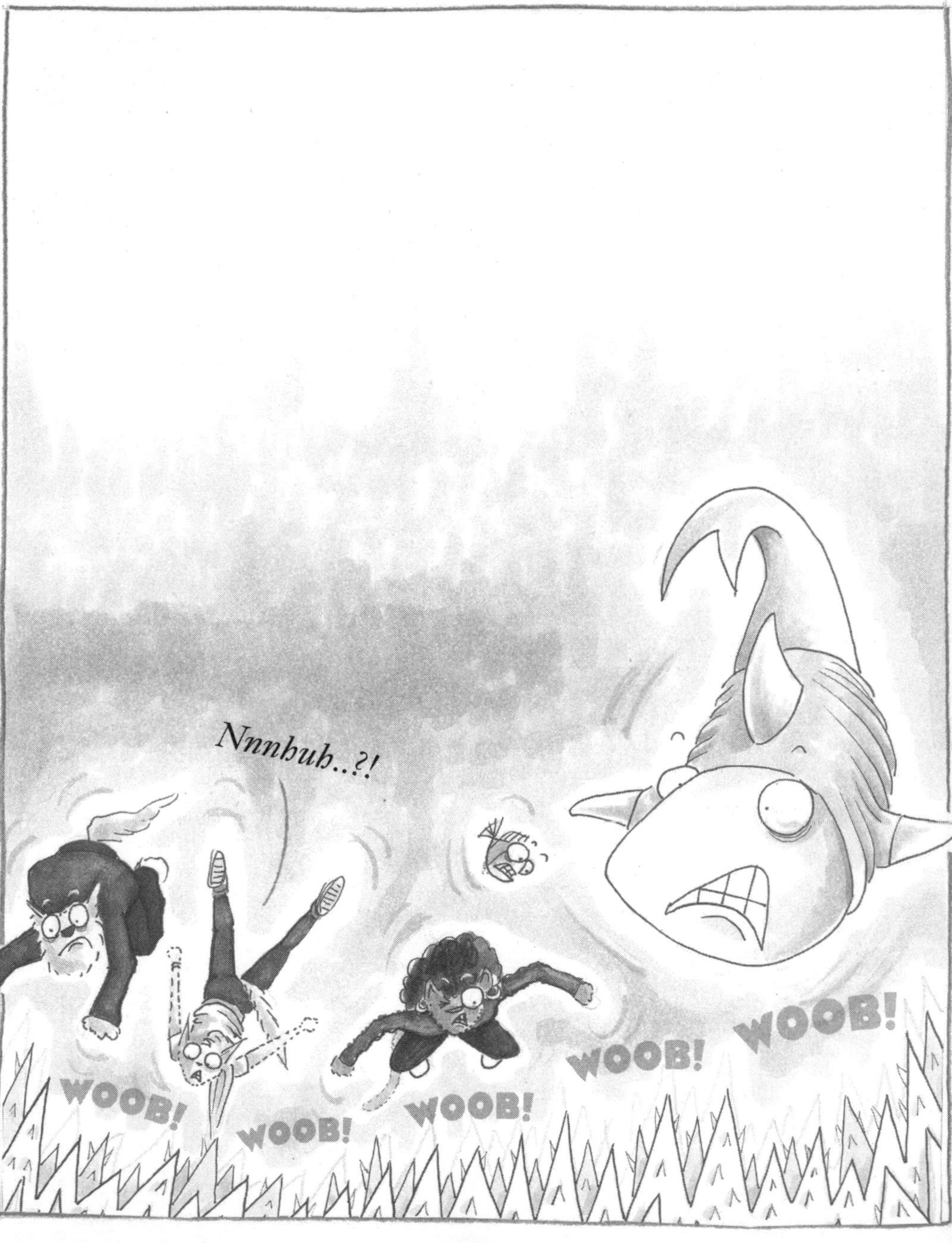
Nnnhuh..?!
WOOB!
WOOB!
WOOB!
WOOB!
WOOB!

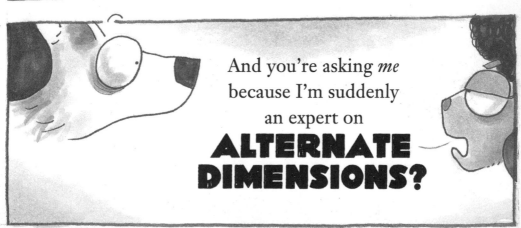

Don't you mean alternate **UNIVERSES?** This is the next universe in the **MULTIVERSE,** isn't it?

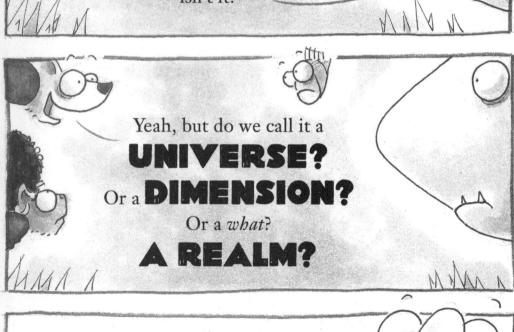

Yeah, but do we call it a **UNIVERSE?** Or a **DIMENSION?** Or a *what*? **A REALM?**

Ooooh! *A REALM!*

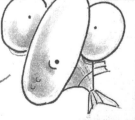

A realm?! You expecting to see dragons and enchanted snowmen and singing squirrels?

They've got *singing squirrels?!*

Look, all I know is we've just fallen through a **PORTAL** into a place that's not in OUR universe. It's a **WHOLE NEW** dimension, or universe, or realm . . .

I vote REALM!

. . . so it's probably going to have some different

GROUND RULES.

Literally.

Get it?

Because we're not touching the gr . . .

My bad.
Too soon.

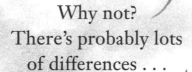

So the
gravity is
different?

Why not?
There's probably lots
of differences . . .

FOOF!

AAARRRRGGGGHHH!!

CHICAS!
WHAT'S HAPPENING?!
WHERE IS *EVERYONE*?!

Piranha, calm down . . .

THE SQUIRRELS ARE HERE!

THEY'RE TELLING ME TO
CALM DOWN!

I thought you said they only
communicated through *song* . . .

It's me, you idiot . . . *WOLF!*

Ohhhh . . . I *thought* that was a
deep voice for a squirrel . . .

Everybody SHUT IT.
Sorry, Agent Kitty Kat . . .
I think this is night . . .
SPLOOF!
OWWWWWWW!

And now it's day again . . .

That was **NIGHT?!**

It lasted about 30 seconds!

How long do the *days* last?!

And what just hit us?!

Why are we covered in bits of jagged, pointy, hard stuff?!

I don't want to know.

Let's just find the

NEXT DOORWAY

and get out of here.

The *next* doorway?! *We just got here!*

Shouldn't we at least look around for the

EVIL
CENTIPEDE-LOOKING
DUDE for a bit?

I mean, how many doorways do we have to go through to find him?!

I don't know
how many.

No-one does.

All I know is that I
have to find . . .

Ooowee!
That never gets old!

He could be
ten more universes
away from here. Fifty more! *A hundred!*

I don't know.

But what I do know, is that he's **NOT HERE**.

So all we can do is find the **NEXT DOORWAY**

and move on to the **NEXT UNIVERSE**.

Wait . . . what?

How do you *know* he's not here?
I mean, this place is pretty horrible.
He *could* be here . . .

He's not.
I can *feel* it.

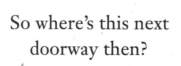

So where's this next
doorway then?

I've been meaning to ask— **HOW** do you guys keep finding these doorways?

I remember seeing the HOT POOP door, but I don't recall how we got there or why we . . .

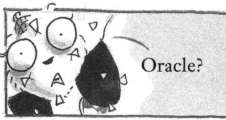

Oracle?

GAK!

Oracle . . . *WHERE IS THE DOORWAY TO THE NEXT UNIVERSE?!*

THIS WAY! IT IS THIS WAY!

FOOF!

Seriously?!

THIS WAY!
IT IS
THIS WAY!

Somebody grab him, will you?

THIS WAY!
IT IS
THIS—

GRAB!

Got him.

Thanks.

Let's just wait until morning.

OK.

SPLOOF!

OWWWWWWW!

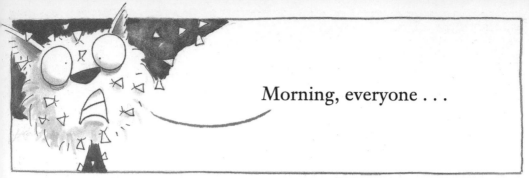

Morning, everyone . . .

THIS WAY!
IT IS
THIS WAY!

And away they go . . .

They're heading right where you said they would . . .

How did you know, dude?

EVERYTHING IN THIS WORLD BELONGS TO UNDERLORD SHAARD.

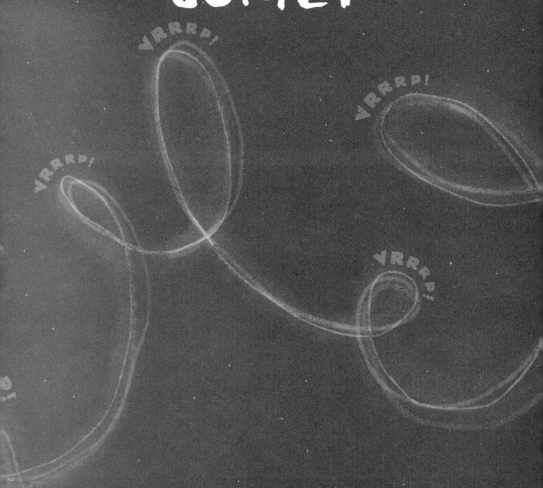

· CHAPTER 2 ·

THE VOMIT COMET

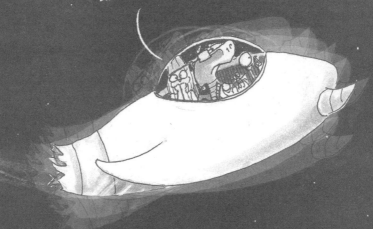

Ah! THE OTHERS! Those *mysterious beings* we need to find on the other side of the galaxy!

Without **THE OTHERS**, Agent Fox—AKA

THE ONE!

—will fail in her quest!

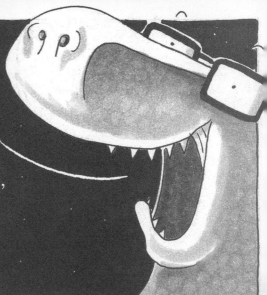

. . . previously on *Milton States the Obvious* . . .

How long will it be, Nathan?

Um . . . about three days . . .

THREE DAYS?!

OF THIS?!

 That's it. I'm throwing up now.

 Yes, I fear I might disgrace myself also . . .

I swear, if any of you losers **BLOW YOUR GROCERIES,** I will pop the hatch and blast us all into *space.*

I MEAN IT!

I have a strong stomach, el Cuervo. Don't worry about me.

I'm *not* worried about you.

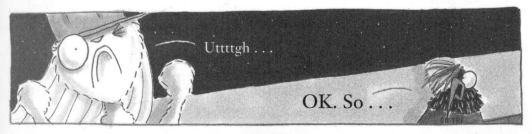

WHAT DO WE DO NOW?!

Uh . . . I might have an idea . . .

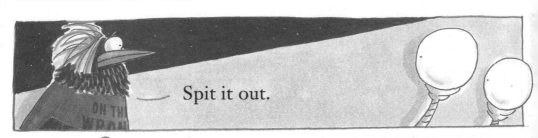

Spit it out.

Bluuuffft?!

Not YOU!

Talk!

Yeah . . . so, anyway . . .
I was thinking . . . maybe we could
ask my **KING** for a **NEW SHIP?**
One that would get us to
THE OTHERS
a little faster . . .

Your KING?
The father of
MARMALADE?

Uh huh . . .

The Marmalade kid who tried to **WIPE OUT OUR ENTIRE PLANET?**

Um . . . yep . . .

You think your monarch would be receptive to such a proposal?

Well, it can't hurt to ask!

It might hurt being blown up by his **WARSHIPS** though . . .

ITEM NOW IN TRANSIT

Title: - The bad guys Episode 13,
Cut

C3059576189

BAD

Pickup location: LHUB

LH - IPS - SBLADE - 02

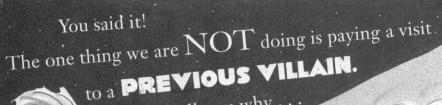

You said it! The one thing we are **NOT** doing is paying a visit to a **PREVIOUS VILLAIN.** And I'll tell you why . . .

Ooooh . . . on second thoughts I *do* feel a little funny . . .

PAPA!

PEPE?!

PAPA! CAN YOU HEAR ME?!
YES, PEPE!
What's up with the old fish?
Does anyone else feel like the
BUS TO HEAVEN
is about to arrive?
OH WRITE

FAAAART!
SPLAT!
What's that smell?!
Is it
Well-Respected-Television-Journalist's
lunch?
GLAAAUUGRRGH!

· CHAPTER 3 ·
FISHY MIND POWERS

GRAB!

So, *thaaat's* how it's pronounced . . .

Duh . . .

HEY! *WHAT'S GOING ON HERE?! DO YOU SMELL THAT?!*

Piranha, were you just talking to your **DAD?**

PAPA'S HERE?! WHERE'S MY PAPA?!

HEY! **HE'S NOT HERE!** THAT'S NOT FUNNY! *DON'T YOU EVER MAKE JOKES ABOUT MY PAPA!*

MUNCH!

AAAARRRGGGHH!

MUNCH!

MUNCH!

He really doesn't know he's doing it, does he?

AAAARRRGGGHH!

No. But if he can get **MESSAGES** to the other team through his papa, that's pretty . . .

MUNCH! MUNCH! MUNCH!

FOOF!

MUNCH! MUNCH! MUNCH!

. . . great.

MUNCH! MUNCH! MUNCH!

MUNCH! MUNCH! MUNCH!

Well . . .
goodnight everybody.

MUNCH! MUNCH! MUNCH!

AND DON'T YOU EVER JOKE ABOUT MY PAPA AGAIN!

SPLOOF!

OK.
Good.

. . . but did he
find the NEXT
DOORWAY, too?

Oh, he found it.

And it's right down . . .

· CHAPTER 4 ·
NATHAN'S WARM WELCOME

I told you
this was a
stupid idea!

Your Majesty!
My name is Commander . . . uh . . Legs . . .
. . and I want you to know that
WE are not your enemies!
Like, AT ALL.
We just need your

HELP!

Who is this?!

He's a spider, Dad. It's an Earth thing. They have eight legs, which is nice, but they also have *BODY HAIR* . . .

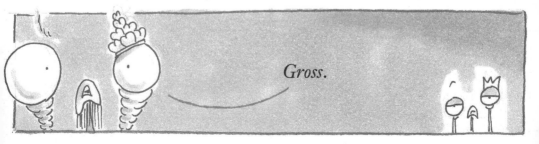

Gross.

BLOW THEM OUT OF THE SKY!

·Wait!·

The **REAL ENEMY** is on the way! Like a totally evil, end-of-life-as-we-know-it kind of enemy!

And if you don't help us . . .

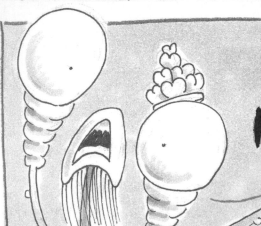

NONSENSE!
My son told us there was
NO DANGER
of such a thing happening!

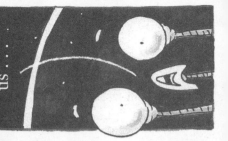

Oooh, no. **TOO MANY CREW MEMBERS.** Once we got on board, they'd slaughter us . . . .

I say, what about **THAT ONE?**

THAT one?!

IT'S THE
PRIDE
OF THE
FLEET!

· CHAPTER 5 ·
DON'T CUT YOURSELF ON THAT

So, what's the play?

WHOO!
And it's got a *kick!*
Whatever you're
gonna do, baby,
DO IT FAST!

BOOM!

What *are* you
going to do?

FOOF!

Oh, just . . . *perfect*.

As soon as the sun comes up again, I want you all to start climbing down . . .

But, Ellen . . .

Wolfie?

Yeah?

Trust me, OK?

OK.

Here goes . . .

SPLOOF!

GASP!

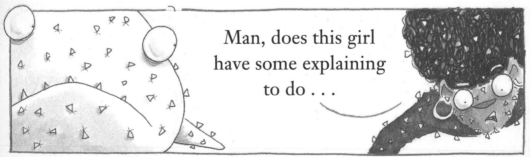

You OK, Emmy?

If you can do **THAT**, sweetpea, this is the *least* I can do . . .

BOOM!

VOOP! VOOP! VOOP! VOOP! VOOP! VOOP!

Told you.
She's, like, *really* good.

THIS IS FOX!
EVERYBODY FREEZE
UNTIL THE SUN
COMES UP!

OK!

Sure!

FFFFFPPP!

Piranha,
did you fart?

Maybe . . .
but that is
my business.

Whoo!
This thing's
getting
heavy . . .

Oh, I think it's far TOO heavy, don't you?

Too heavy . . .

They're just **USING** you. You don't *neeeeed* them . . .

SPLOOF!

IT'S **SNAKE!**
AND THE CANNON!
SHE LET GO OF THE CANNON!

GIVE UP NOW, FOX,
AND I'LL MAKE THAT
CANNON
DISAPPEAR...

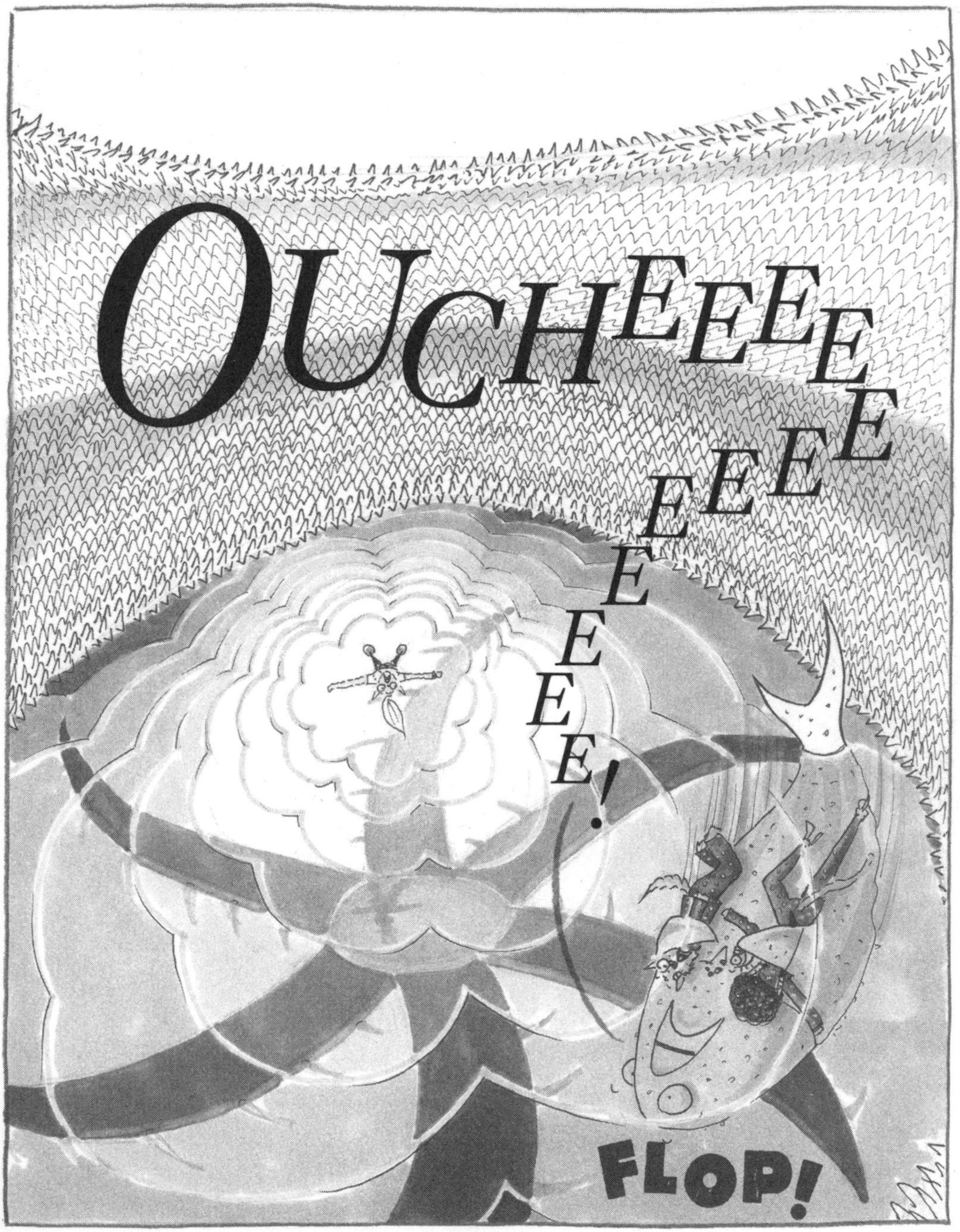
OUCHEEEEEEEEEEEEEE!
FLOP!

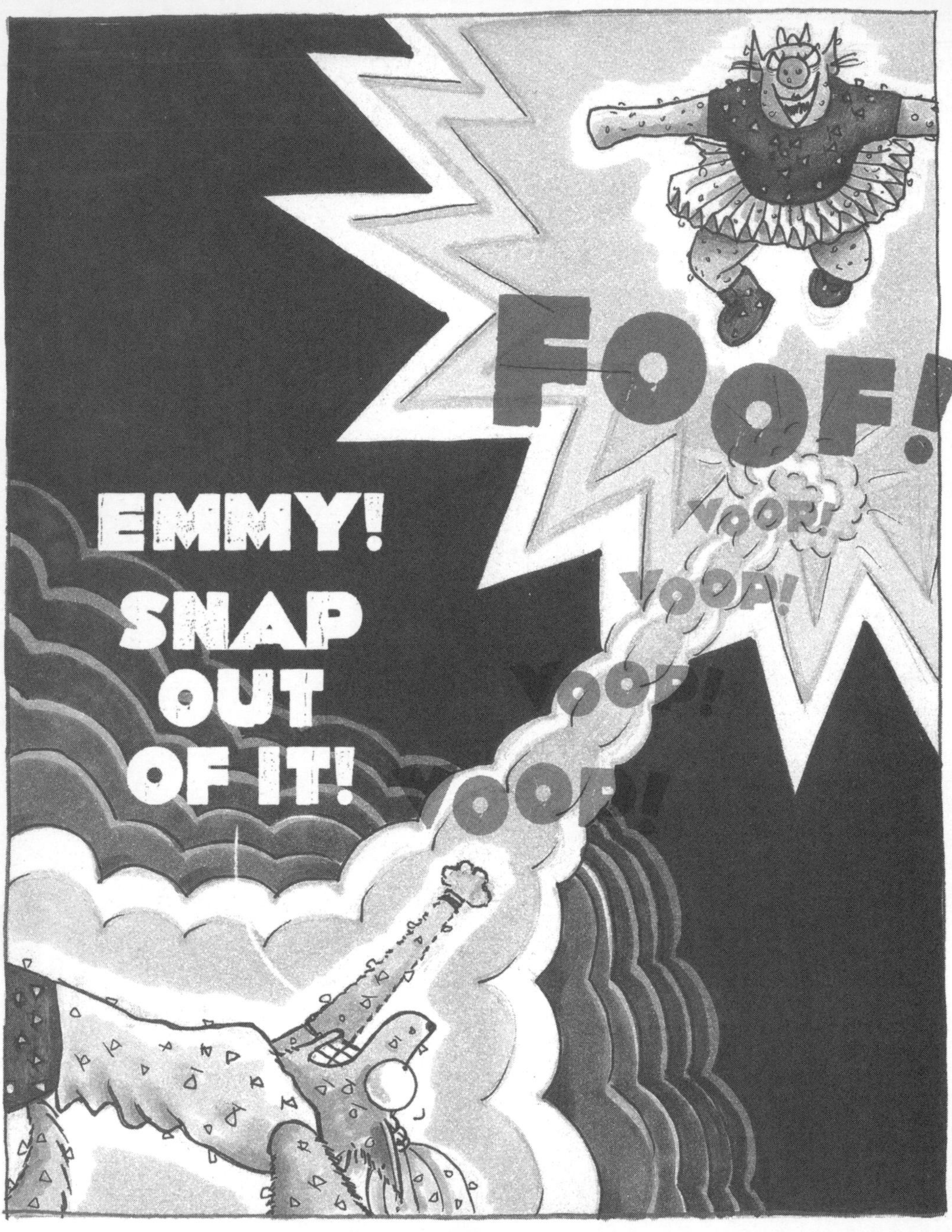
FOOF!
VOOP!
VOOP!
EMMY! SNAP OUT OF IT!

HAHAHA!

It's . . . not . . . working . . .

CAN YOU FEEL HOW MUCH STRONGER I'VE BECOME?!

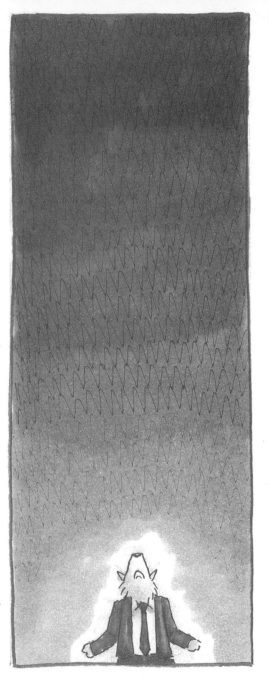
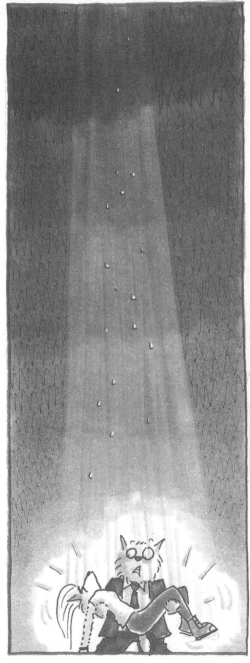

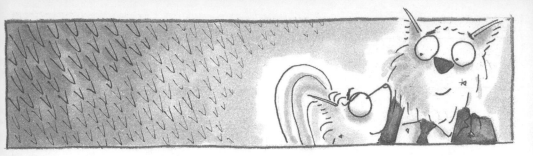

 Thank you . . .  NOD

OW!

Nearly done.
Just a few more
shards . . .

Sharky! Oh, my big, beautiful Sharky! **WHAT DID I DO?!**

What did you do?! You let that cannon fire right at his big old . . .

· CHAPTER 6 ·

MAKING THE UNIVERSE BEAUTIFUL

It's a big old butt,
is what it is.

It's a

GARBAGE FREIGHTER,
actually.

It was designed to resemble a
HAND—a hand that gathers waste,
making the universe beautiful.

It's quite a nice thought, when you
think about it that way . . .

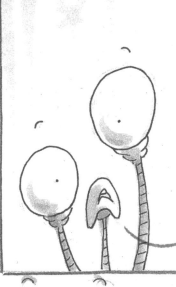

Is it in tip-top condition, though?

BRRPt!

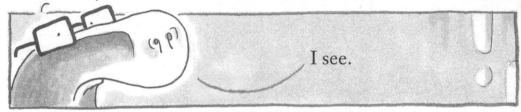

I see.

THEY KNOW WE'RE IN HERE! THEY'RE COMING! GET US OUT OF HERE!

Okey dokey.

THRUSTERS TO FULL...

FFFFT!

THAT'S IT?!

With the thrusters at FULL?

What's wrong with it?!

Hang on,
I think the
FUEL RODS
are dead.

Hmmm. Yep.
We need a top-up.

A TOP-UP?! *What?*
Are you saying we need a
GAS STATION?
Where can we find
a gas station?

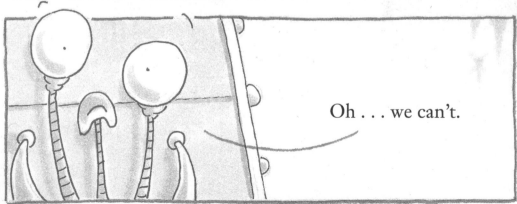

Oh . . . we can't.

What?

... 'cause it looks like you guys sure could use some help.

CHAPTER 7

TOO EASY

EVERYONE, LISTEN UP!

Emmy, Shark's right—it *wasn't* your fault.

It was **SNAKE**.

But I need you all to understand something—
Snake is getting STRONGER.

He got hold of you, Emmy,
and, for a minute there . . .
I was certain . . .
I couldn't get you back.

This is getting serious,
guys. If he gets any
stronger, I won't be able
to keep him from . . .

TURNING you.

So, what are we waiting for?

FREEZE!

You don't think it's a little

TOO CONVENIENT

that we can all suddenly *walk again*?
Or that the ground is now
magically *safe to walk on*?
That doesn't set off
any alarm bells?

Nope.

I mean, the **DOORWAY** is just . . . there. Easy, right?

That *IS* the doorway, isn't it, Piranha?

That's what they tell me . . .

And that doesn't seem **TOO EASY** to you?

Do you really think they'd leave their precious doorway **COMPLETELY UNPROTECTED?**

It *looks* unprotected. That's all I'm sayin'.

Uh huh.

Well, whatever they've got waiting for us, I say . . .

· CHAPTER 8 ·
UNBELIEVE-A-BULL

I'm just a guy who loves to **PARTY**...

Are you?

Perhaps the question was too difficult. I'll ask it louder—

WHO ARE YOU?

You mean *him*, right?

I mean,
do you see
anyone else
with, like,
seven butts?

Ah, just to clarify,
these are actually
HANDS and . . .

GOOD GRIEF! You've really given this vessel some **OOMPH!**

YEAH! LET'S GO!

WAIT A MINUTE!

We don't even know who you are!

WHY are you helping us?

HOW did you arrive EXACTLY when we *needed* help?

WHY would you **PUT YOURSELF IN DANGER**, like this?

WHAT DO YOU ACTUALLY WANT, MAN?!

WHO ARE YOU?!

HEY!
Do ya trust me?

No.

Not
at all.

Not
even a
little.

I
really
want
to.

THEN LET ME PUT
IT TO YA LIKE THIS—
**YOU'RE ON A
MISSION, RIGHT?**

Um . . .

Well . . .

We
probably
shouldn't
say . . .

Kiiiiiind
of . . .

 AND EVERY MISSION NEEDS **A LEADER, RIGHT?**

 Um . . .

 Technically . . .

 That's true, but . . .

 OMG, *YES!*

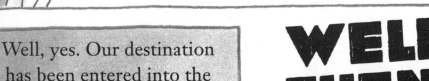 THEN, BUTT GUY, **DOES THE SHIP KNOW WHERE TO GO?**

Well, yes. Our destination has been entered into the navigation system . . . but I'd like to make it clear that these really are *hands* and . . .

WELL THEN, LISTEN UP!

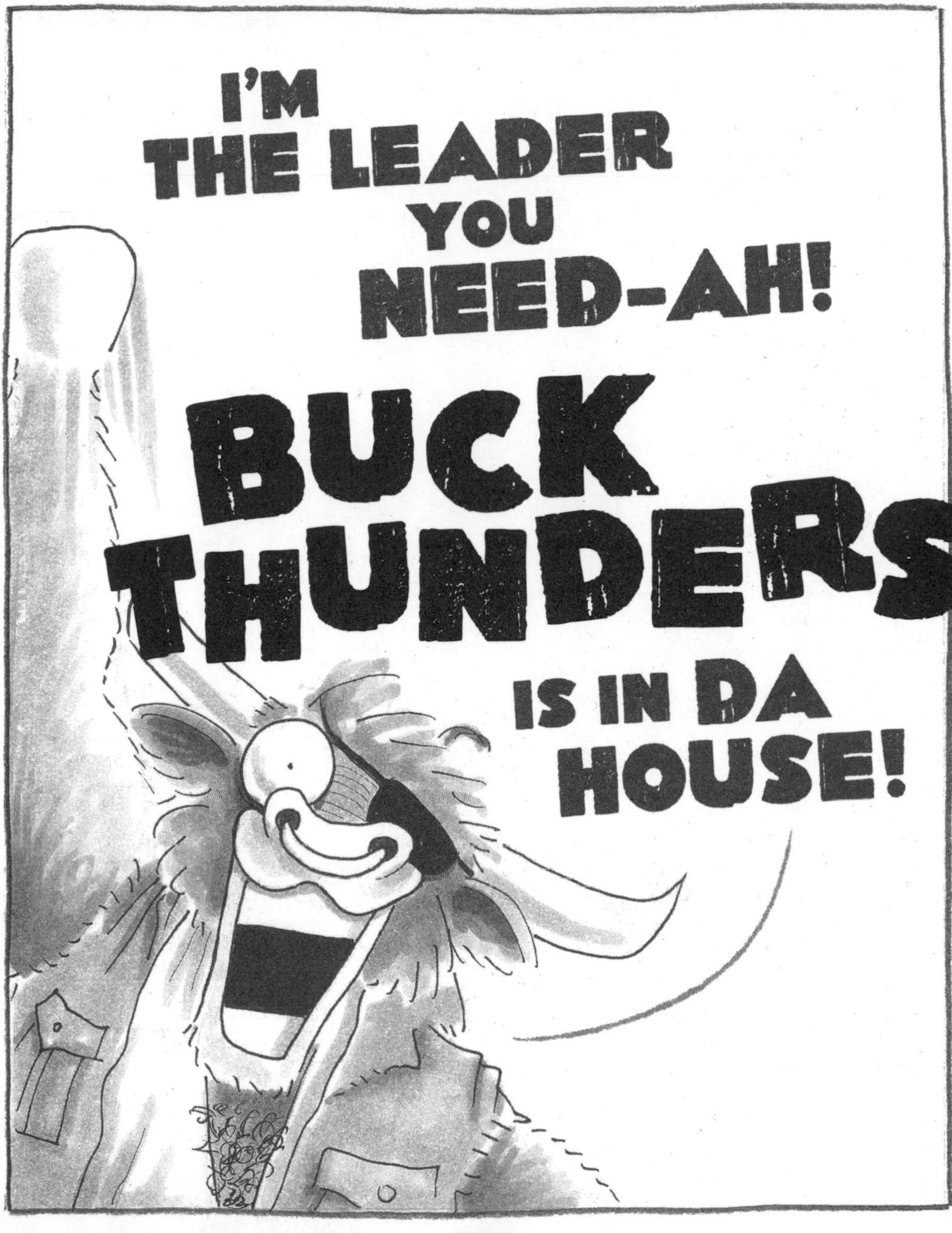
I'M THE LEADER YOU NEED-AH!
BUCK THUNDERS IS IN DA HOUSE!

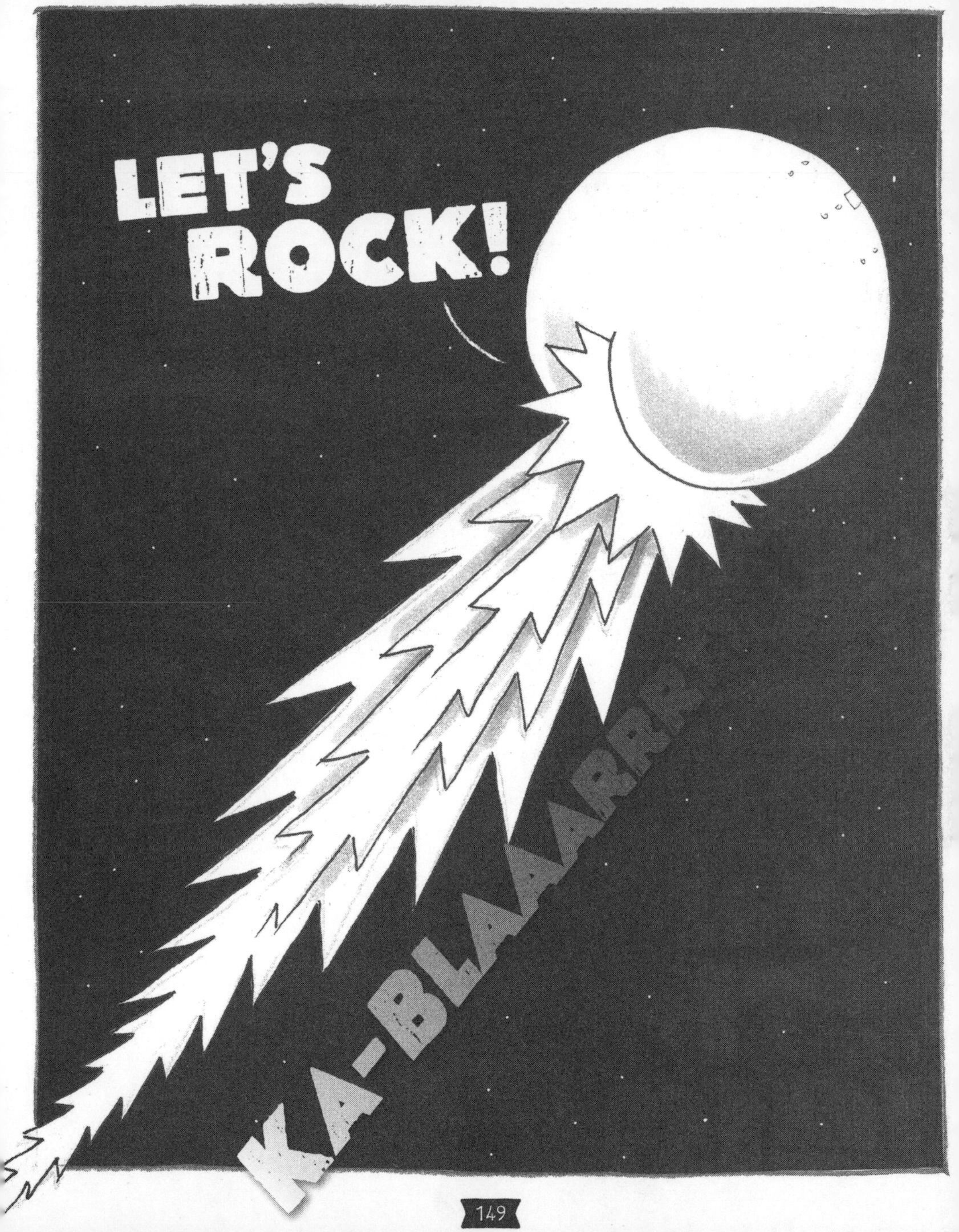
LET'S ROCK!
KA-BLAAARRR

· CHAPTER 9 ·
VRING NING NING!

May I introduce

UNDERLORD SHAARD.

VRRING! NING!

NING!

Suddenly butt-hands don't seem so bad . . .

But *MY POWER* **FEEDS ME!**

*MY POWER IS BETTER THAN **YOUR** POWER!*

SO YOU CAN'T WIN THIS ALL ON YOUR OWN.

For once, I agree with him.

FLING!

SNATCH!

I just wish you'd shut up occasionally.

NING!

NING!

KITTY!
NO!

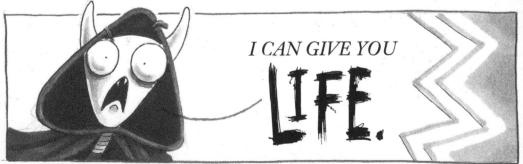

Wolf, talk to your boy, will you?

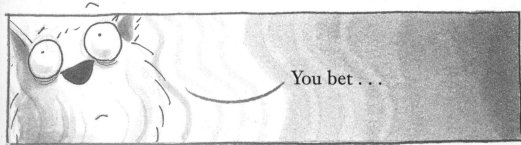

You bet . . .

Hey there, little buddy . . .

YOU NEED TO LISTEN TO ME!
I DON'T WANT TO HURT YOU!
I DON'T WANT TO HURT ANY OF YOU!
BUT THEY DO!

After all we've been through, you really don't know?

Buddy, I'd rather **DIE GOOD** than **LIVE BAD.**

And the Mr Snake I know would say the same . . .

GRAB!

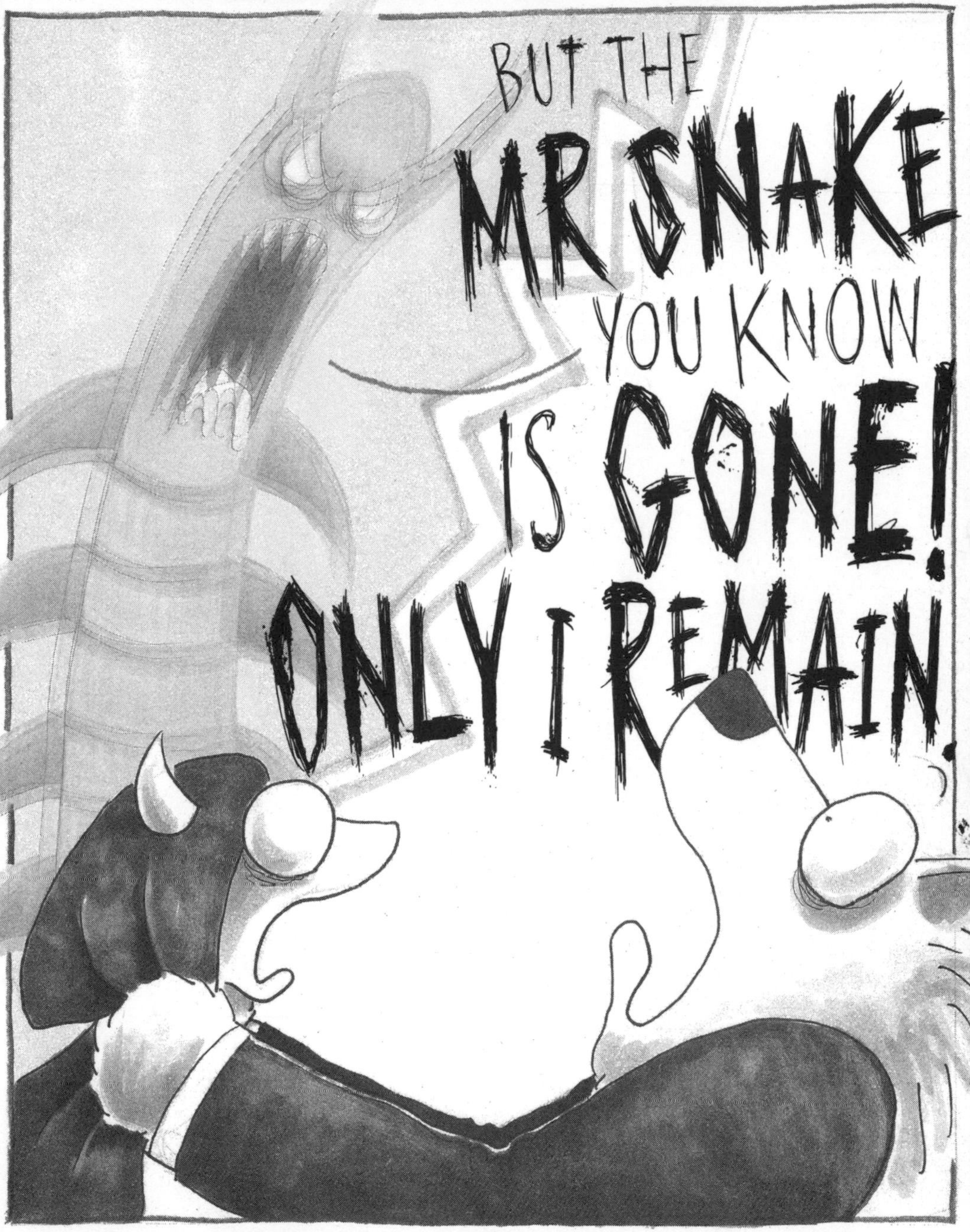
BUT THE
MR SNAKE
YOU KNOW
IS GONE!
ONLY I REMAIN!

I know this is bad,
I do, *I know*,
but *that* is
OUTRAGEOUS...

AND YOU ARE THE ONE. NOT WHAT I EXPECTED. YOU LOOK EASY TO DESTROY.

LEAVE
MY BUDDY
ALONE!

WOLFIE!
YOU'RE TOO CLOSE!

DESTROY
THEM ALL!

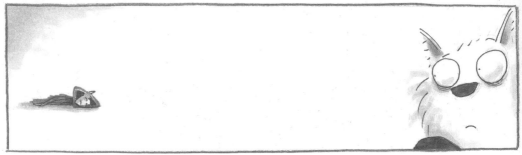

Ugh . . .

Wolf?

· CHAPTER 10 ·
LONG WAY DOWN

Or not . . .

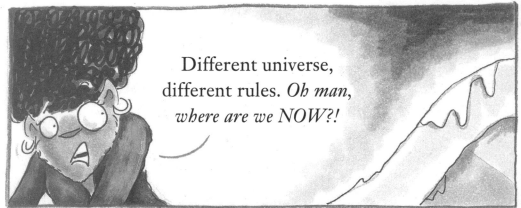

Different universe,
different rules. *Oh man,
where are we NOW?!*

Ellen! *Wake up!*

She doesn't look good . . .

Piranha, where's the **NEXT DOORWAY?**

How should *I* know?!

How hard can *that* be?

TO BE
CONTINUED . . .

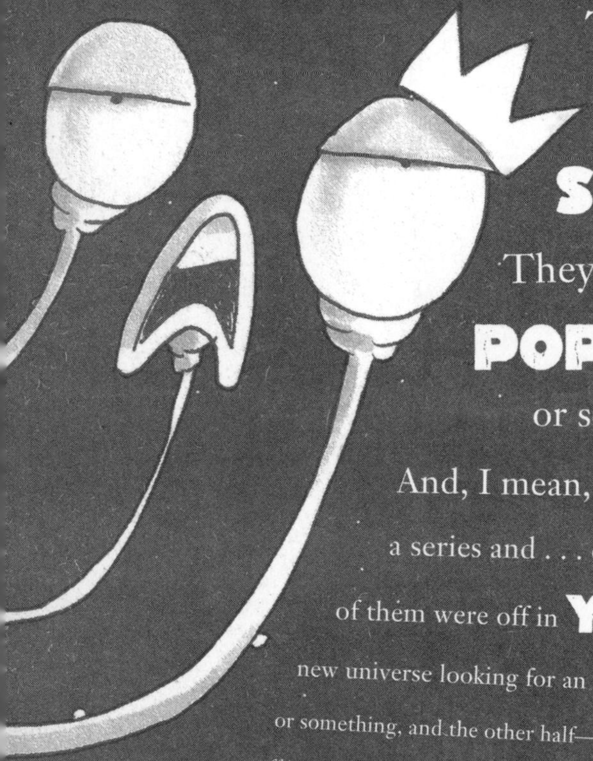

So, like I told my dad . . .
it's **ALL COOL,** babes.
NOTHING to worry about.
Those Earth guys
are just being
SO DRAMATIC.
They behave as if their life is a
POPULAR SERIES
or something, you know?
And, I mean, EVEN IF their life **WAS**
a series and . . . oh, I don't know, let's say HALF
of them were off in **YET ANOTHER** weird
new universe looking for an **EVIL CATERPILLAR**
or something, and the other half—let's call them THE B-TEAM—
were off in space with a suspiciously pushy one-eyed bull, looking for some vague but
weirdly intriguing new characters they call **THE OTHERS** . . .
well . . . EVEN THEN . . .
There'd be ABSOLUTELY NO REASON to read th—

the BAD GUYS EPISODE 14!
COMING SOON!